For Jessica

Love is "forever and ever!"

EX LIBRIS

This Book Belongs to

_____

# My YELLOW BALLOON ™

### BY Tiffany Papageorge

### ILLUSTRATED BY ERWIN MADRID

MINOAN
MOON
PUBLISHING

"No! It's supposed to hurt—
that's how you know
it meant something!"

~ Peter and the Starcatcher


"No love, no friendship, can
cross the path of our destiny
without leaving some mark
on it forever."

~ François Mauriac

For the Balloon Man
and for my amazing family,
Paul, Demetri, Timothy, and Arianna,
who he tied to my heart.

∼ TP

For my mom and dad,
Felicitas and Silvano

∼ EM

At last! The carnival had come to town.
Joey dashed through the grand entrance.
His parents could barely
keep up with him.

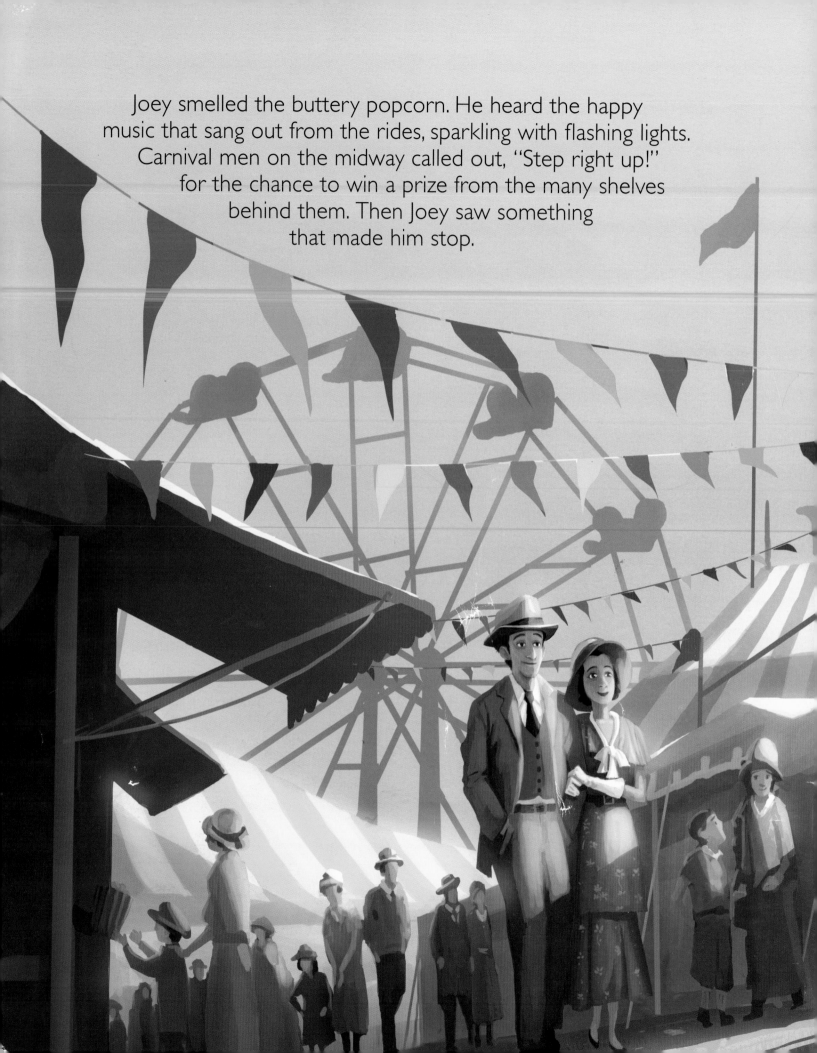

Joey smelled the buttery popcorn. He heard the happy
music that sang out from the rides, sparkling with flashing lights.
Carnival men on the midway called out, "Step right up!"
for the chance to win a prize from the many shelves
behind them. Then Joey saw something
that made him stop.

Hundreds
of big, bright
balloons floated,
as if enchanted,
in the air like
a cloud of many
colors. Slowly,
Joey walked
up to them.

The ripe old man drew Joey in with his deep voice.

"Would you like a balloon?" he asked.

"Oh yes sir!"

"Which one, Joey?" his mother asked.

"Um, I don't know." Joey said, mesmerized.

"This is your balloon Joey."
Without even looking
up, the balloon man pulled
on one of the many strings
and out sprang a bright
yellow balloon.

The balloon man wrapped the string around Joey's wrist and said, "Here, let me tie you two together."

From that moment on, they were never apart.

Every morning the summer sun skipped through Joey's window and the birds sang their wake up song, eager to see the two buddies running through their adventures.

The bees,
neighborhood dogs, and
old oak trees enjoyed
watching them play
day after day.

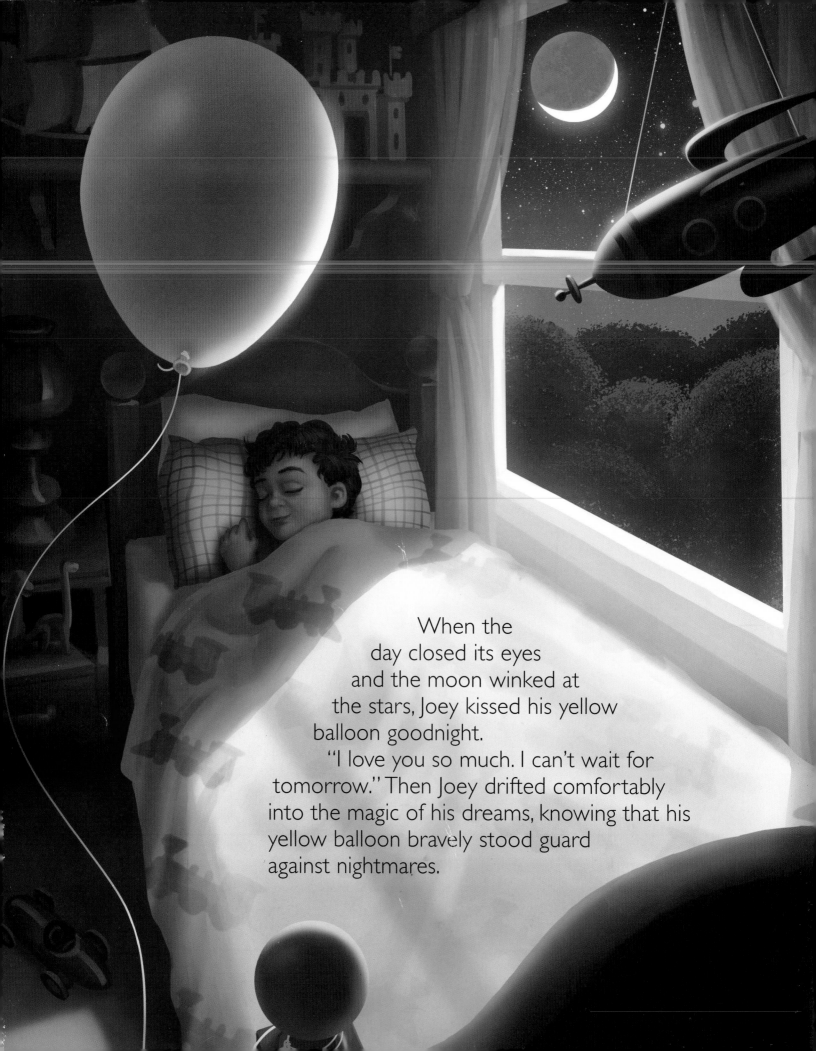

When the
day closed its eyes
and the moon winked at
the stars, Joey kissed his yellow
balloon goodnight.
"I love you so much. I can't wait for
tomorrow." Then Joey drifted comfortably
into the magic of his dreams, knowing that his
yellow balloon bravely stood guard
against nightmares.

Then one day

in one second

everything changed.

Joey and his yellow balloon were
playing and somehow, some way,
it slipped off his wrist.

It began to float away before Joey knew what was happening.

"Come down!" Joey called out.
His yellow balloon reached out its string
with all of its might but it couldn't come down.

Joey ran to find his mother.
   "My, my, yellow balloon! It's gone," Joey sobbed.
   "Oh sweetheart," she said. "Let's go get you
   a new toy. That will make you feel better."

"No! All I want is my yellow balloon. Get it back,"
Joey demanded. "Please! I'll do anything if you get it back!"
"I wish I could," she said.

Joey stormed into his room
to be all by himself.

Joey felt **angry.**

He felt **confused.**

He felt so very **sad.**

"I wish you would come back," Joey sighed.
He cried and cried and cried some more. He cried
so hard he fell into a dream, so real . . .

In his dream, Joey's yellow balloon was with him
and they both started to fly . . .
past the rustling trees . . .
past the soaring birds . . .
past the mountain peaks
and into the depths
of Joey's universe.

Far away he heard . . .

"Wake up, Joey. Dinner's ready."
He opened his heavy eyes. He remembered his yellow balloon was gone and tears came tumbling out again. His mother and father held him close until he felt safe and loved.

The rest of the summer Joey missed his yellow balloon all of the time.

Then one day he was sad *most* of
the time instead of all of the time.

As time passed, he was sad *a lot* of
the time instead of most of the time.

Then the day came that Joey felt sad
only *some* of the time.

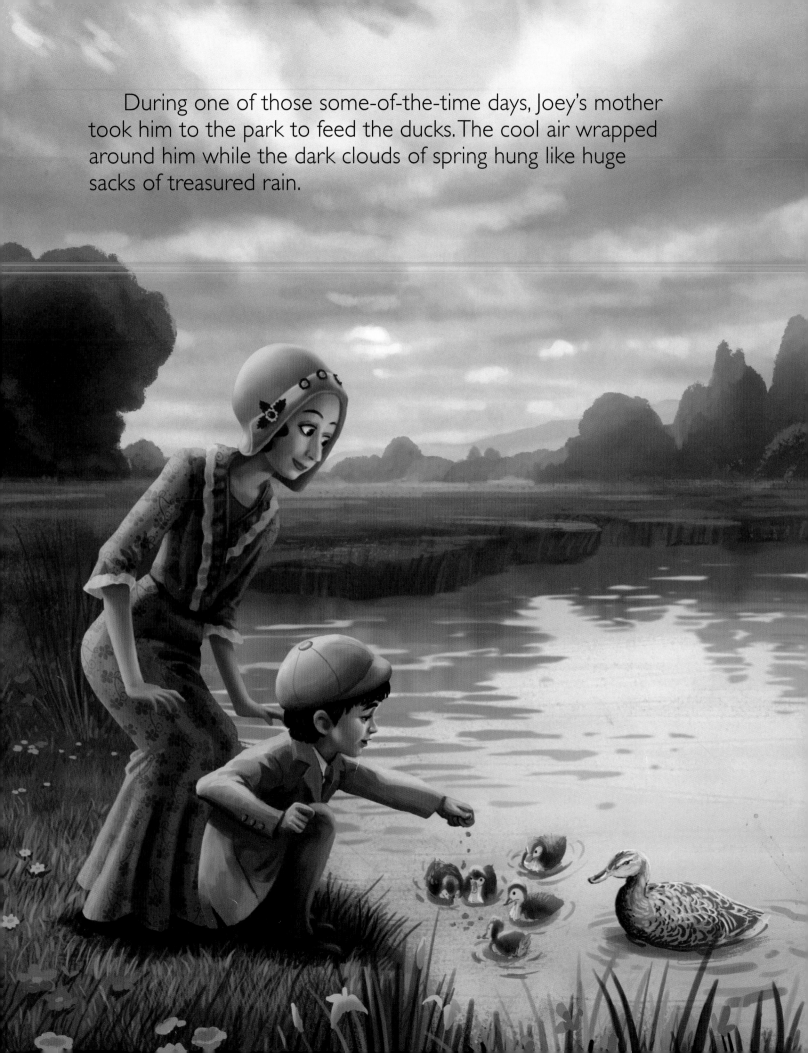

During one of those some-of-the-time days, Joey's mother took him to the park to feed the ducks. The cool air wrapped around him while the dark clouds of spring hung like huge sacks of treasured rain.

Joey felt something warm and tingly on his back. Something caught his eye in the water. It was bright and yellow. Joey's heart did a fast somersault in his shirt!

"My yellow balloon?" he whispered.

Joey spun around
and looked up. It was so
bright he couldn't see.
He reached to grab its
string and pull it to him.
But there was no string.
It wasn't his yellow balloon
at all. It was the sun.

It had been so long since Joey noticed the sun.
It reminded him so much of his yellow balloon
he had to smile.

Once more

in one second

everything changed.

Tenderly, the sun warmed him.

"I still miss you," Joey said. "But, whenever I see the sun, big and bright, I'll feel you with me. Wherever I am, wherever I go, you are a part of me and I am a part of you. We're a part of each other forever and ever."

Thank you to those, both here and beyond,
who have inspired and touched this story along the way.

Published by Minoan Moon Publishing
100 Pine St., Suite 1250
San Francisco, CA 94111

Illustrated by Erwin Madrid
Edited by Rebecca McCarthy
Book Design by Michael Rohani

Publisher's Cataloging-In-Publication Data

Papageorge, Tiffany.
My yellow balloon / by Tiffany Papageorge ; illustrated by Erwin Madrid.

pages : illustrations ; cm

Summary: Joey goes to the carnival and makes a new friend: a bright yellow balloon. Joey
and his beloved balloon do everything together, until the balloon accidentally slips
off Joey's wrist and flies far, far away. What will Joey do without his special friend?
A tale of love, loss and letting go that serves as a comforting guide for children
who are navigating the complicated emotions of grief.
Interest age level: 003-008.

ISBN: 978-0-9903370-0-3

1. Balloons--Juvenile fiction.  2. Friendship--Juvenile fiction.  3. Loss (Psychology) in
children--Juvenile fiction.  4. Grief in children—Juvenile fiction.  5. Balloons--Fiction.
6. Friendship--Fiction.  7. Loss (Psychology)--Fiction.  8. Grief--Fiction.
I. Madrid, Erwin.  II. Title.

PZ7.P363 My 2014
[E]

Printed in the United States of America
10 9 8 7 6 5 4 3 2
First Edition